Becky's Special Folder

By Jay Sanders

Illustrated by Suzie Byrne

Chapter 1

All Alone

It was time for recess.
Becky sat all alone on the school playground.

She got up and walked slowly over
to some girls playing under a tree.
"Can I play with you?" she asked.

"No," said Amy. "There are no seats left."

Becky walked away.
She was sad and very lonely.

3

Becky's teacher, Mrs. Wills, came over.

"Becky," she said,
"do you have a friend to play with today?"

"No," said Becky.

"Our school garden looks very dry,"
said Mrs. Wills.
"Would you like to water the flowers
for me?"

"Yes, please," said Becky.
"I help Mom in our garden at home."

Becky helped Mrs. Wills until the bell rang.

Chapter 2

Mom Helps Out

After school, Mom came to get Becky.
"How was school today?" she asked.

"Good," said Becky.

Mom looked at Becky.
She could see tears in her eyes.

"Mom," said Becky,
"last year I had some friends,
but this year I don't have any friends at all."

Mom gave Becky a big hug.
"Let's think of something you can do,"
she said.
"You could go to the library at recess
and help Mr. Jacob with the books."

"But, Mom," said Becky,
"the library is not open at recess."

"I know what you can do!" said Mom.
"I will give you a special folder
with some new paper and pencils in it.
When you are lonely,
you can sit at a table outside
and do some drawing."

"Thanks, Mom," said Becky,
as she rubbed away her tears.

Chapter 3
A New Red Folder

The next day,
Becky took her new red folder to school.

When the bell rang for recess,
she took her folder outside
and sat at a table.
She got out her paper and pencils
and started to draw.

Some girls from Becky's class came over.

"What are you doing?" asked Kristy.

"I'm drawing a picture of my dog," said Becky.

"Can I draw with you?" asked Kristy.

"Yes," said Becky.
"Here is some paper for you."

"Can I draw, too?" asked Emma.

"Yes!" said Becky.

After school,
Becky came running over to Mom.
"I had a *very* good day!"
she said with a big smile.
"Kristy and Emma sat with me at recess
and did some drawing.
We are going to draw some pictures
tomorrow, too.
And Emma has asked me
to come to her house on Saturday
to see her new goldfish."

Mom smiled and gave Becky a big hug.